CW00985135

Stanley
the tale of the Lizard

by PETER METEYARD

Pictures by PETER FIRMIN

ANDRE DEUTSCH

Lizards are now tiny, but in King Arthur's time

There were big ones they called dragons, and told about in rhyme.

This is the tale of a gentle Knight and a girl with gleaming hair,

And how he was helped to win her hand by a dragon in his lair.

First published 1979 by
André Deutsch Limited
105 Great Russell Street London WCI

Text copyright © 1979 by Peter Meteyard
Illustrations copyright © 1979 by Peter Firmin
All rights reserved

Colour reproduction by Culver Graphics Litho Ltd
Lane End Bucks
Printed in Great Britain by Hazell Watson & Viney Ltd
Aylesbury Bucks

British Library Cataloguing in Publication Data

Meteyard, Peter
    Stanley, the tale of the lizard.
    I. Title   II. Firmin, Peter
    821'.9'14   PZ8.3

    ISBN 0-233-97071-1

First published in the United States of America 1979

Library of Congress Number
78 74466

King Arthur was quite famous for his thousand and one knights

Who sat at his round table, and boasted of their fights;

How in the lists they'd canter up, then gallop down the course

With lances set to jar the other knight from off his horse.

Then, when he'd fallen off it, how they'd wheel and gallop back

With sword or mace or axe or chains . . . to finish the attack.

With revelry and pageantry, the days passed quickly by,

For all except Sir Lance-a-little who was rather shy.

He didn't like the revelry,

    he couldn't stand the noise;

And he'd rather ride around his farm

    in comfy corduroys.

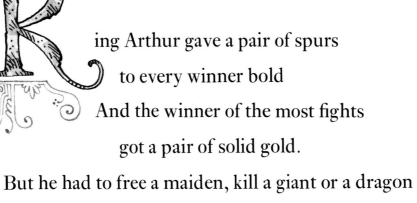

King Arthur gave a pair of spurs

    to every winner bold

  And the winner of the most fights

    got a pair of solid gold.

But he had to free a maiden, kill a giant or a dragon

Or capture on his own a castle with an ogre's flag on.

Sir Lancey said, "I'll never win. I'd very quickly scoot

From an ogre or a dragon and then I'd get the boot."

For the horse whose knight in deadly fight

   should flinch or funk or fail

Had to carry his lord for a year and a day

   with a jack-boot tied to his tail.

Now Stanley was a dragon;

    the largest of his kind.

Ten fathoms from his muzzle to his scaly tail behind.

And though his drink was water,

    his food, I must confess,

Was baby calves and lambs and things,

    and damsels in distress.

His breath was central heated,

    So no knight could venture near

But if he coughed or sneezed at all he always shed a tear

'Cos he burned his pocket handky up, which meant he had to fight

To appropriate another from some most reluctant knight.

Well, baby Stanley drank from pools, but then as he grew up

The streams and lakes would disappear,

    his hot breath dried them up.

His fiery breath soon scorched his throat

and then his thirst was frantic

Till he wandered down to Cornwall

where he found the broad Atlantic.

At first he drank from ripples and then he found that waves

Were salty and refreshing; and look at the time it saves!

But what's he saving time for? And what do dragons do?

Well they must earn their living, the same as me and you.

So Stanley, in a cavern, set up a blacksmith's forge

Repairing scales for dragons perforated by St George.

Now perhaps you think that dragons never lived, or very few,

And none at all like Stanley. Well just in case you do

I'll tell you now how Lance-a-bit met Stanley face to face

While thinking hard of something else and falling fast through space!

He travelled down to Cornwall.

he went by horse, of course.

His horse, of course, was a courser,

that's a coarser horse – of course.

He doffed his weighty armour
  and in his shorts and vest
Went climbing down the cliffs
  to find an oystercatcher's nest.

To help him keep his footing on the perpendicular rock
He used his sword, which he'd adapted as an alpenstock.
But unlike alpine climbers he'd no rope to hold him tight
And suddenly he slipped and fell from a most ghastly height.

He closed his eyes and dropped his sword

and wished he hadn't come.

Then landed with a bump

and bounced and bounced

till he was numb

On something soft but scaly

which he later found to be

The cliff end of the dragon

who was facing out to sea.

At last he finished bouncing, and was running down the beach

When the dragon turned to catch him

   but found he simply couldn't reach,

He pulled, but – ow! – his tail was stuck, for Lancey's alpenstock

had pierced the softer, hinder end, and pinned it to the rock.

So Stanley called to Lance-a-bit and said,

"Hang on old sport,

Your climbing stick's gone through my tail;

   I'm well and truly caught.

I promise I won't hurt you if you come and set me free

And I'll give you anything you want in payment of a fee."

The knight crept back beneath the cliff

   and wrenched the blade away.

Stanley turned to thank him

   for his good deed for the day,

And they walked the beach together to the dragon's sunlit cave

Then Stanley said, "A boon is yours; what metalwork you crave

I will execute this minute, as it's getting rather late,

In Cornish copper, steel or tin, or gold or silver plate.

"So have a cup of coffee, I will make it for you gladly.

There's no need to look so wistful, or to sigh so very sadly."

But Lancey whistled to his horse and said, "No, never mind,

I'm afraid the metalwork I want is rather hard to find.

It requires a lot of courage,

    and you cannot give me that.

So good afternoon. . ."

    His horse came in, he took and raised his hat,

Which was, of course, a metal one. When Stanley saw the mail

He said, "Why you're a knight, sir, do you seek the Holy Grail?

Because, of course, I can't make that, but if you seek the Spurs,

As most knights do who roam abroad, a plan to me occurs.

And as for courage, you'll find out there are no other men

Who have talked to and had coffee with a dragon in his den."

ust find a maid," the dragon said, "and tie her to a rock.

Then say you'll be back later

   when you've had a glass of hock.

Then I'll go up and roar at her, and give her such a fright

That she'll scream for you to save her,

   and become her faithful knight.

And when you charge upon the scene

   with polished armour gleaming,

I'll be glad to leave you hastily . . .

   I can't stand maidens screaming."

ost maids," said Lance, "are chained to rocks,

    for sea-serpents to eat them,

Or in guarded bread-and-water towers,

    where parents soundly beat them.

And it's very very difficult, unless you have the key,

To think of any clever way to ever set one free.

ut still," said Lance, "I'll take a hammer,

    staples and some chains

Along the beach and find a rock, in fact I'll spare no pains."

So Lance-a-little trotted off along the sandy strand,

With chains across his saddle-bow and pliers in his hand.

ust as he was coming round a corner to a bay

He heard a sniff and saw a maid as in the reeds she lay.

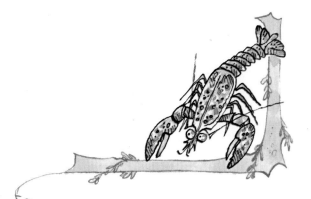

He drew rein with a tinkle. The lady, startled, rose.

She smoothed her dress, tossed back her hair,

    and quietly blew her nose.

The chains slipped from the saddle and brought Lancey back to life.

He hadn't often talked to girls, and hadn't got a wife.

So he said, "Do please sit down, miss.

    This may come as quite a shock,

For I've brought these chains to tie you

    to that seaweed-covered rock."

Then Lancey picked the longest chain with a padlock on to lock it

And took the pliers, hammer and some staples from his pocket.

He tied the maiden firmly, then he got up on his horse.

He galloped off for breakfast, which was very rude of course,

And the maiden felt quite lonely; she was just about to cry,

For she wasn't used to knights who left and didn't say 'goodbye',

When another knight in armour black

appeared the other way,

And when he saw the maiden tied

he laughed and said "Hooray!

'll take her to my castle which is only half-a-mile."

Then he levered out the staples with a jemmy and a smile.

As Lancey neared the dragon's cave he heard the dragon yell

"Here's your coffee. You'll excuse me,
    for I'm off to drink as well."

Then he bounded down the foreshore
    before Lancey could explain

About the maiden that he'd found
    and tied up with a chain.

Drinking coffee from his helmet

   which the dragon used to brew it,

He thought about the dragon's plan,

   and hoped that he could do it.

Then he set off down the beach . . .

   but the dragon, from the sea

Had already seen the maiden as she struggled to get free.

So he swished and swished his tail about and gave a fearful roar

And like a flying catfish made a beeline for the shore.

The black knight's charger saw him and, with a whinney, fled

With the black knight tight upon his back. They left the maid for dead.

But Stanley hotly chased the knight right up the cliff so high

The path led straight for the castle gate

   but the frightened horse went by.

It went so fast it galloped past and galloped off the cliff.

Stanley skidded over too . . . now he was frightened stiff.

He dug his five-toed claws in, but he simply couldn't stop.

He landed on the knight below and heard

    him go off POP!

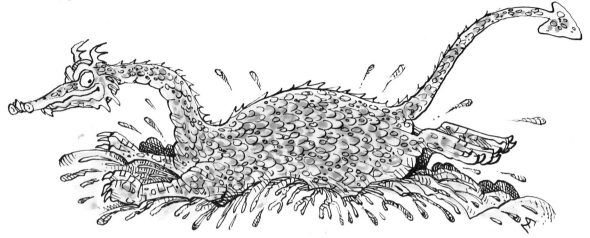

His blood stained all the rocks there,

    you've no need to dig a mine.

You can see them on the beach still and they call them Serpentine.

Stanley got up shaken, then saw the charger dead.

Ah, just what I need for dinner. It'll give me strength," he said.

The King was counting all the spurs the other knights had won

When Lance-a-bit walked in and said, "I've had a bit of fun.

Won't you come and see my dragon

and the maiden that I've freed?

The dragon's killed the black knight

and gobbled up his steed.

So now his castle's empty

and I think I'll farm down there.

Then Stanley will have friends and food

not too far from his lair;

And I'd like to marry Gloria (that is the maiden's name),

She's friendly with the dragon, he really is quite tame."

"You've done all this?" said Arthur. "You really are quite zealous.

Look at Lancelot and Tristram there,

   and Galahad . . . they're jealous."

And that's the end.

   The black knight's castle rang to happy laughter.

Stanley kept them warm in winter.

   They lived happy ever after.

King Arthur died in later years, in spite of Merlin's magic,

And so did Lance and Gloria. But the end is not all tragic.

Stanley keeps vigil by their tombs, as only dragons can

For dragons are immortal and don't have to die like man.

So there he lives beneath the rocks,

    where he built Lancey's grave,

And he never needs to go out now for the tide comes in his cave

And mermaids bring him lobsters – and crabs he rather likes.

He says the shells are good for him and harden up his spikes.

He boils the sea in winter time all round the Cornish coast,

And I think of dragons I have known

    he's the one I love the most.

the end